Victoria OSTEEN

Gifts from the Heart

illustrated by Diane Palmisciano

Little Simon Inspirations
New York   London   Toronto   Sydney

"My name is Princess Sue," said Sue.
"And you're a knight, Sir Jon.
Here is your sword, and here's my crown.
Please help me put it on."

"Now see that kingdom over there?"
inquired Princess Sue.
"I think those children need our help.
Let's see what we can do!"

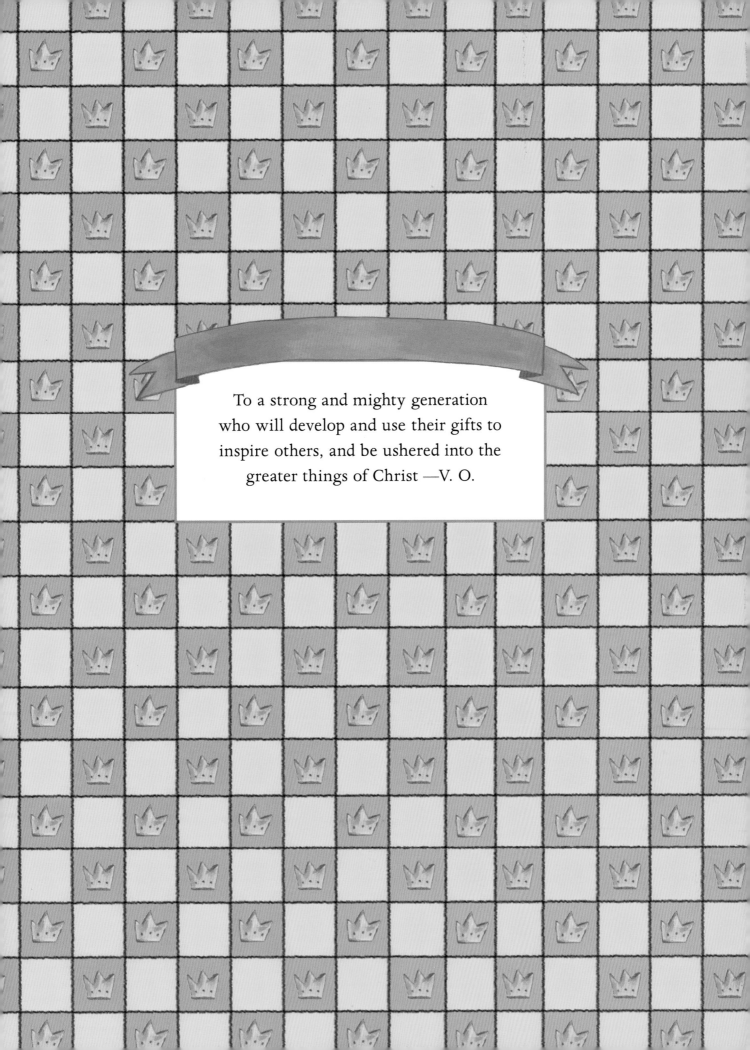

To a strong and mighty generation
who will develop and use their gifts to
inspire others, and be ushered into the
greater things of Christ —V. O.

LITTLE SIMON INSPIRATIONS • An imprint of Simon & Schuster Children's Publishing Division
1230 Avenue of the Americas, New York, New York 10020 • Copyright © 2010 by UGT PARTNERS, LTD. • All rights reserved, including the right of
reproduction in whole or in part in any form • LITTLE SIMON INSPIRATIONS and associated colophon are trademarks of Simon & Schuster, Inc.
For information about special discounts for bulk purchases, please contact Simon & Schuster Special Sales at 1-866-506-1949 or
business@simonandschuster.com. • The Simon & Schuster Speakers Bureau can bring authors to your live event. For more information or to book
an event contact the Simon & Schuster Speakers Bureau at 1-866-248-3049 or visit our website at www.simonspeakers.com.
Manufactured in the United States of America 1010 PCR • Design by Laura Reddick • 10 9 8 7 6 5 4 3 2
ISBN 978-1-4169-5551-1

4

"Excuse me, please," the baker said, as he rushed right past Sue.
"I have to bake a royal cake. There's just so much to do. . . ."

"What's going on?" asked Princess Sue. "Why are the streets so busy?"
"It must be something big," said Jon, "'cause folks are in a tizzy!"

"It is a party for our king," explained a girl nearby.
"Tonight the kingdom celebrates . . ." Then she began to cry.

Royal Bash for the King
...NEST Gifts Accepted

"It's been announced: To meet the king,
we must have gifts to bear.
But I've no gold to buy a gift,
no way to show I care."

"You do not need to cry," said Jon.
"I'm here to help with Sue.
I'm a knight, and this is my horse,
the strong and fearless Lou."

"What is your name?" asked Princess Sue.
"I'm Mary Anne," she said.
"I have no riches to be shared—
No crown upon my head."

"You do not need a crown," said Sue,
"to give a gift that's true.
The finest gifts in all the world
God put inside of you."

"But there's a law," said Mary Anne. "It passed just yesterday.
The King's assistant, Robbie, said: 'Bring gifts or stay away!'"

"Well, if Sir Robbie keeps us out," Sir Jon said with a grin.
"We'll celebrate right here, right now! C'mon we'll all pitch in."

"We'll pool our talents," said Sir Jon. "Together, we'll do great!
We'll have a pageant for the king to celebrate this date."

"Hey, I can juggle," said one boy. "And I can twirl!" said Sue.
"That's great!" said Jon. "Now, who can paint? We've got a lot to do!"

The children worked all afternoon. They even built a stage.
But when Sir Robbie heard the noise, he stormed out in a rage!

"Just what is going on?" he yelled. "Today is King's big day!
You're making quite a lot of noise. Shoo! Shoo! Now go away!"

"Please do not make us leave," said Sue. "We've worked hard all day long.
We're here to celebrate the king—with puppets, art, and song!"

"But you can't come to our big bash," Sir Robbie harshly said.
"We know," said Sue. "That's why we planned our party *here* instead."

"So be it, then," Sir Robbie said. "But do not make a scene.
If you disturb the king tonight, I might have to get mean!"

"Don't worry, friends. Just do your best!" Sir Jon said with a smile.
"Just use the talents God gave you. Let's do this thing in style!"

Some kids practiced their twirling dance.
Some juggled fruit real high.
Some made a special sign that said:
"Oh, King, you're quite a guy!"

But Mary Anne could not juggle,
nor dance, nor paint a thing.
So feeling sad, she hummed a bit.
Then she began to sing.

The children listened to her voice
as it began to lift.
"God put a song in you!" cried Jon.
"That's it! That is your gift!"

At six o'clock the sign went up,
and then the show began.
The children sang their song of love
alongside Mary Anne.

They sang a song so beautiful.
Its notes soon reached the king.
He followed it into the street,
amazed by everything.

The king walked right up to the stage,
and no one said a word.
He asked, "Who has done all of this?
Who sang that song I heard?"

"Oh, no! Oh, no!" Sir Robbie said.
"I told these kids: 'No noise!'
I'm sorry, King. I'll deal with this.
Now go home, girls and boys!"

But then Mary Anne stepped out in front and curtsied left and right.
"My friends and I did this for you . . . I hope it is all right."

"We so wanted to honor you," she said, bowing her head.
"We could not buy you fancy gifts, so we did this instead."

The king reached down and took her hand and said, "You're very sweet.
Each one of you gave from your heart and made this day complete."

"Our work is done," said Princess Sue.
"You rock! Great job, you guys!
Sir Jon and I must leave you now,
so we'll say our good-byes."

She turned to Mary Ann and said,
"I have something for you."
She placed a crown upon her head.
"You're a princess through and through."

"I have something to give you too—
it's from our hearts," said Jon.
"We hope you like our special gift.
Please share it when we've gone."

"Good-bye! Thank you!" said Mary Anne, as she unrolled the note,
"These words are for each one of us. And here is what they wrote:

*Always live by these Kingdom Thoughts. They'll keep your joy alive.
And always share your special gifts. They'll help your kingdom thrive!*

KINGDOM THOUGHTS

You may not wear a golden crown,
but you are royalty deep down.

Together we can
do big things.
We can touch the
hearts of kings!

Always listen to what's in your heart.
Then you'll know just where to start.

Though you are young, you can do much.
Just think of all the lives you'll touch!

Just give your best
in all you do.
Your gift will make
a way for you.

ROYAL Q & A

1 Mary Anne didn't think she had anything to give the king, but then her friends pointed out that she could sing really well. What gifts do you have to share with the world? How can you share them?

2 Princess Sue and Sir Jon helped Mary Anne and her friends put on a show to honor the king and didn't expect anything in return. Why do you think they did that? In the end do you think they received something in return anyway? What was it?

3 The kids in the kingdom worked together to put on a show for the king. Have you ever worked together on something big? Why is teamwork so important?

4 What's the best gift you've ever received? Why? What's the best gift you've ever given?

5 On the opening pages 4-5 you'll see many items in Jon and Sue's playroom that appear later in the story. Have fun finding them!

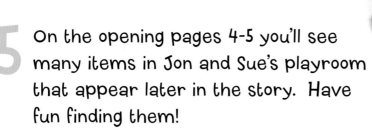

"A gift opens the way for the giver and ushers him into the presence of the great." —Proverbs 18:16 (NIV)

You are God's special treasure, and he has put greatness on the inside of you. As you journey through life, allow your gifts and talents to lead you, and God will open great doors of opportunity. As you share your gifts you will inspire others to use theirs. Remember to give your best in all you do, and your gifts will make a way for you.

—V. O.

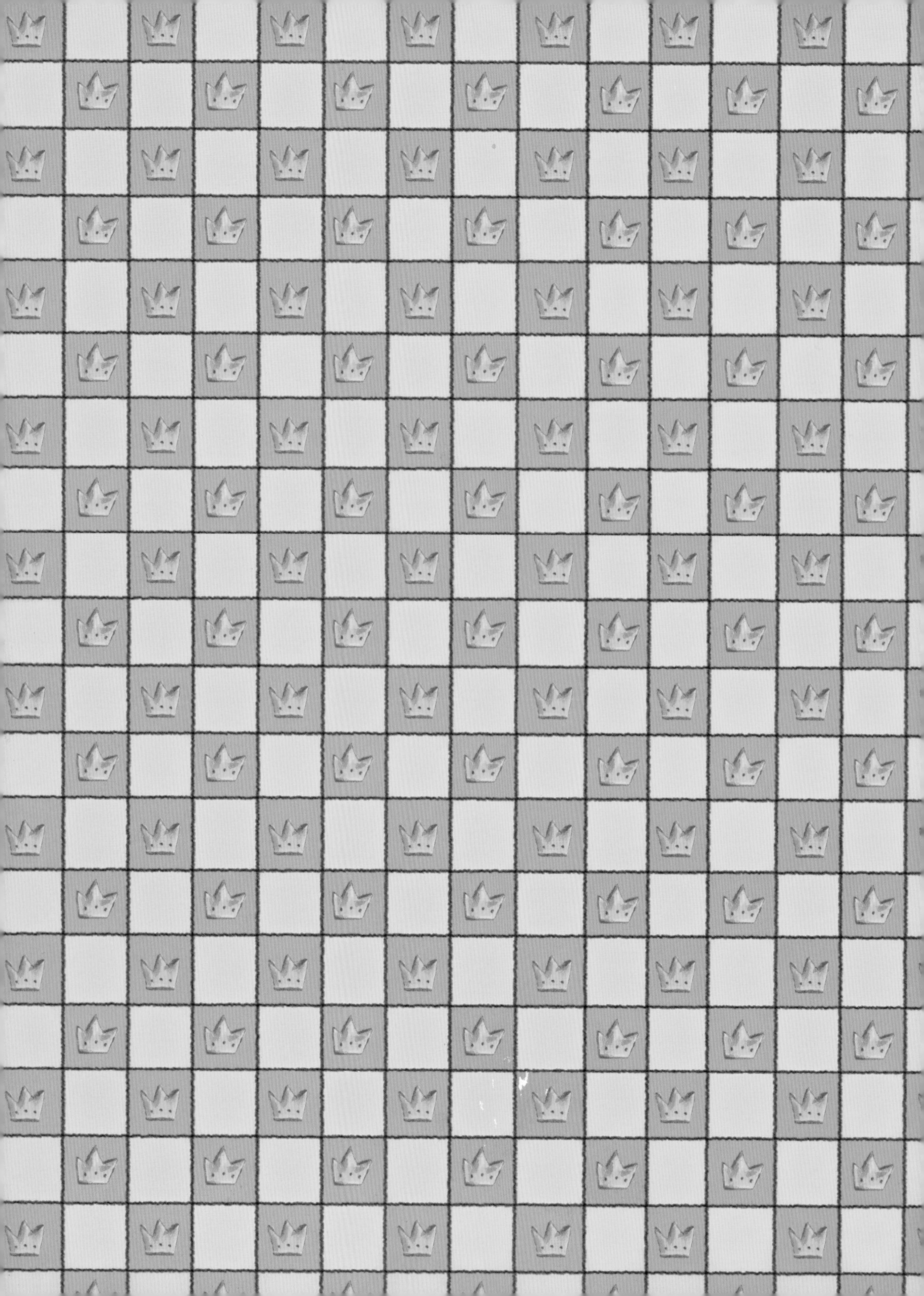